# THE GYMNAST

BY NADINE A. LUKE

Library of Congress Control Number: 2020921219

978-1-7350635-6-0 Hardback
978-1-7350635-7-7 Paperback

# Dedication

This book is dedicated to my daughter Adia and
all of the children who have ever aspired to
release their greatness!

I'm a gymnast and I want the world to know it! I know you're probably thinking, "You're too young. You're only five! What do you know about being a gymnast?"

Well, I know that I can do the best cartwheel better than any other five-year-old in my whole kindergarten class.

When I'm in the grocery store, my mom always says, "Adia, get off of the railing. That's not what that's used for...Baby, stop doing those cartwheels. You're going to hurt yourself!"

At school, my teachers always say, "Adia, cartwheels aren't allowed in school! Adia, it's someone else's turn to get on the monkey bars."

I could stay on those monkey bars all day. I even created special gloves to help me hold on longer.

My teachers all say these things because they don't know it yet.

I'm going to be the world's greatest gymnast ever!

You want to know how I know? It's because I love tumbling and flipping and my parents said I can be anything I want to be!

You should see me! When I'm in the front yard of my house, I have an entire audience—my two dogs, Shorty and Pinky, the dogs across the street, and all of the adults come out to their front yards just to see me!

Okay, well maybe they come out because it's trash day. But they still can't wait to see what I'm going to do next. They all stop and watch me—the gymnast.

After my performance, everyone oooh's and aaaah's and says, "Wow! When are you going to the Olympics?" I just smile and say, "Thank you! I'm too young right now, but soon!" They smile back and we all laugh.

My mom and dad smile and shake their heads. My dad picks me up, looks me in the face and says, "One day, Adia! You ARE the world's greatest gymnast and one day the whole world will know it!

I know my parents really believe in me because the day after I turned five, they took me to this huge building filled with all the things I saw when I watched the Olympics on TV! I looked around full of excitement!

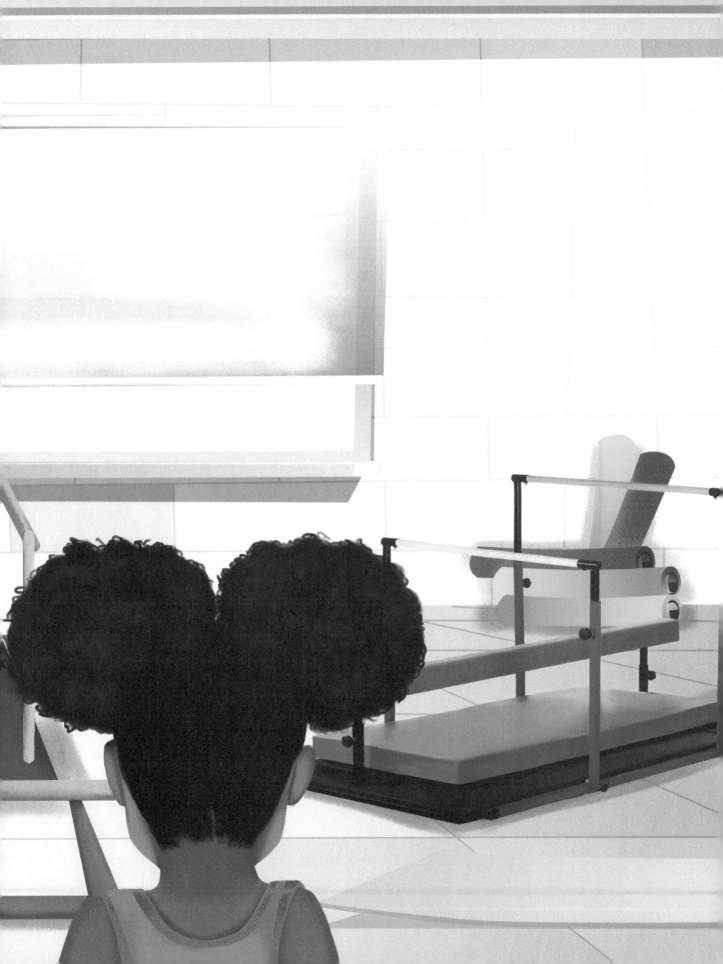

My parents introduced me to my new coach, Ms. Dawn. She bent down and spoke to me in a soft voice, "I heard you are the world's greatest gymnast! Welcome to our gym. We are happy you chose to join our team."

I smiled from ear to ear!
I was so glad someone else knew it too. I turned to my
parents and said, "I'm going to love it here!"

"Do I start now?" I asked my mom and dad. When they said yes, everything in the gym started calling my name. The balance beam, the uneven bars, the trampoline, and the floor chanted, "Adia, try me first!"

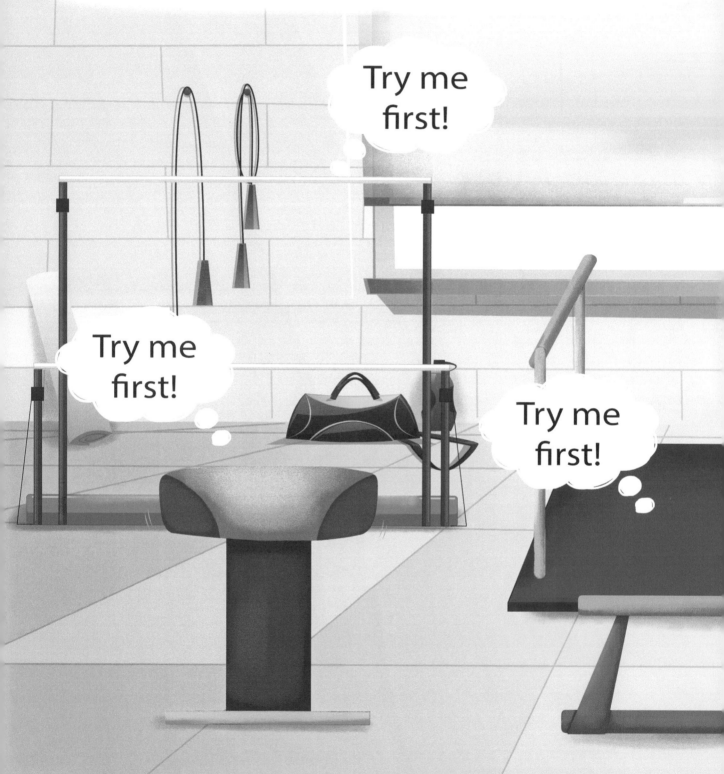

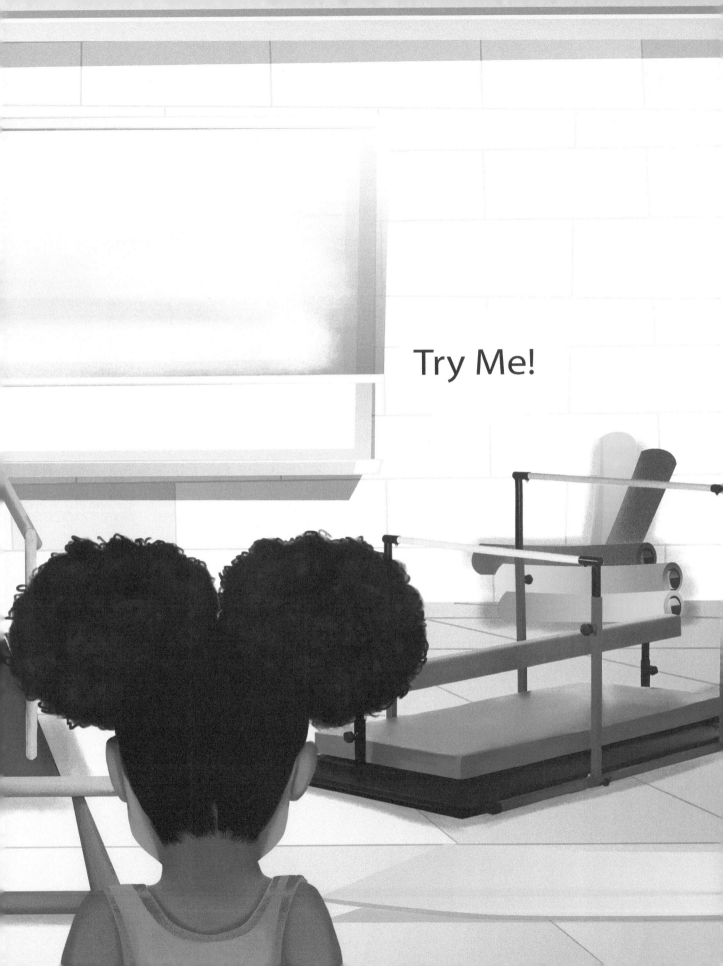

They had five different types of trampolines and they were all different from the small round one in my backyard. Coach Dawn interrupted the chant by telling me to join the other gymnast on the floor for warm-up.

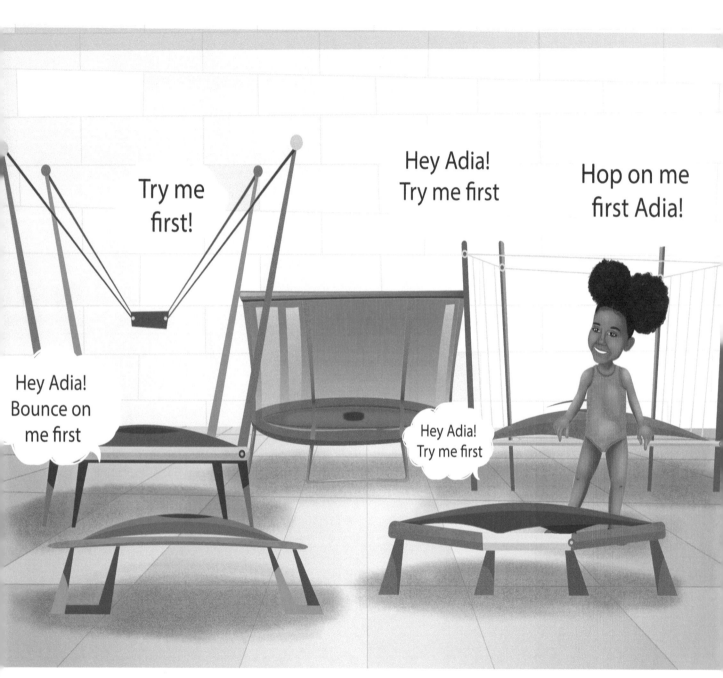

I didn't want to warm-up. I wanted to show her everything I could do. After all—the trampoline was calling my name the loudest!

My coach didn't seem too interested in what I could do.
She had us stretch, do some other funny looking things,
and run around the room.

All the while I kept looking at the trampoline, the foam pit, the bars, and the balance beam wishing I was on one of them.

After a while, my prayers were answered! Guess where I got to go first? The trampoline!

I was ready to show them all of my cartwheels and rolls.

I wanted them to see why everyone in my neighborhood called me the trampoline queen! Only we weren't doing cartwheels on the trampoline. She had us hopping.
Surprisingly, I still had fun acting like a bunny rabbit.

When I did a cartwheel my coach said, "Not yet, Adia.
But look at you! That's a nice cartwheel."

I smiled and beamed with pride. I couldn't wait to show my coach everything I could do.

At the end of practice, Coach Dawn told my parents what a good job I did on everything!.

It was definitely a day to remember.
I was so tired when I got home that I could
barely keep my eyes open.

While eating dinner my head kept falling. My brother and sister laughed when my face landed in my potatoes.

At that point my mom decided to get me ready for bed.  Once I was bathed and all of the mashed potatoes were off my face, she and my dad tucked me into bed.

The next morning at breakfast I couldn't wait to tell everyone about my first day in gymnastics with Coach Dawn! They were hanging on to my every word!

Well, what can I say?

I love gymnastics! Now it's time for everyone to know that I am the World's Greatest Gymnast!"

Lightning Source UK Ltd.
Milton Keynes UK
UKHW051319221222
414334UK00003B/13